The Smell of Poo
Children's Book Collection

All **Five** 'Smell of Poo' Children's Books

Plus 2 bonus 'Pooems'

By Peter Allerton

www.peterallertonwriter.blogspot.co.uk

DEDICATION

This Children's Story Book Collection is dedicated to the Poohglet, friends and family - they know who they are - and my home City of Liverpool.

'The Smell of Poo'
Children's Book Collection

For more weird and wonderful stories, please visit my blog:

www.peterallertonwriter.blogspot.co.uk

The MisAdventures of Mr & Mrs Poo

For the purpose of the telling of this story, 'Pooglish' has been translated into English for two-legged monsters to read.

Chapter Poone: Born

Mrs and Mrs Poo were born in a very special way. They came from a big, hairy, smelly dog's bottom. It was a very smelly bottom indeed.

'Phew,' said Mrs Poo, 'I'm glad that's over - it was like a dog's bottom in there!'

'That's because it was, my sweet' Mr. Poo said, landing with a bit of a splat. 'I'm just happy we didn't get stuck in its tail!'

They watched the dog, their dog, walk away and looked at each other. To anybody else, they just looked like small brown sausages with stumpy little arms and legs. But to Mr Poo, his wife looked like a queen, with nice big eyes and lips, while she thought he was simply the handsomest thing in the world.

They then looked around in amazement at the little country lane where they had landed. 'Where do you think we are?' Mrs Poo asked.

'I have nooo idea. Hey, maybe that poo over there can tell us.' Mr Poo pointed to another poo which had also just landed nearby on the pavement.

'Great, another poo! Ok, let's go and say hello' suggested Mrs Poo. But just as she was speaking, a great big two-legged monster bent down, put the poo into a bag and carried it away! It was quite a scary looking creature, with long arms and legs and a bunch of hair at the top. It looked quite dirty to the Poos.

'Oh, that poor poo, I wonder where it's being taken by that big ugly thing' worried Mrs Poo as she watched nervously. 'I don't think it's safe around here at all!'

'I think you might be right about that, darling,' agreed Mr Poo, trying to hide the fear in his voice. 'We've spent our whole lives cuddling happily inside a nice and comfortable dog's bottom. But now what are we supposed to do?'

'Hey, maybe we can find another dog's bottom to hide inside?' Mrs Poo wondered.

'Ah, that's a fine idea!' Mr Poo gave his wife a big squelchy hug, then shouted 'Look out!' and threw her onto the ground.

Out of nowhere, a gigantic pair of two-legged monsters came running towards them. The Poos froze on the spot, terrified. The monsters were moving too fast for them to get out of the way.

'Eurgh, dog poo!' one shouted as she saw the Poos right in front of them. 'Argh!' screamed the other, jumping over Mrs Poo.

The monsters looked behind them as they carried on running. 'That's horrible, I nearly ruined my new jogging shoes!' 'Yuck!' the Poos heard them say.

'Hey, less of the horrible thank you, *that's my wife!*' Mr Poo angrily shouted after them.

Chapter Ptwooh: Thirsty

'Phew, that was a close one! Maybe from now on we should just keep still if we see any more of those big ugly monsters.' Mrs Poo said. 'I don't want to be squashed into a flat thing, I want to stay lovely and sausage-shaped for my handsome husband.' She winked at Mr. Poo and started posing like a model.

He blushed bright brown. 'Wow! Ok then, let's get out of here. I don't want anything squishing my beautiful queen!'

He gave her a quick kiss and off they squelched along the pavement, leaving a little trail of poo behind them. The Poos enjoyed looking at all the plants and flowers and huge buildings and big moving metal things and everything else around them as they went along the little lane.

A short while later they began to slow down. 'I don't feel so good. I'm thirsty' complained Mr Poo.

'Oh dear, you're starting to lose your lovely colour. You're turning... white!'

'White? *White?* But I'm supposed to be b-b-brown!'

Mrs Poo looked up at the sun. 'It's that big yellow thing up there, it's too hot. We're drying out!'

The Poos were turning more and more pale and becoming slower and slower.

'Urgh, this is terrible' complained Mr Poo, nearly falling off the edge of the pavement and into some flowers. 'Hey, hold on, look through there' he croaked. He pointed through the flowers towards a little stream running past the lane. 'Water, we can go for a swim!'

'Great, like being on holiday or something!' cheered Mrs. Poo, trying to wave her dried out arms in the air.

So the Poos climbed through the flowers, held hands and jumped down together, splashing into the stream. They then started floating along it.

'Aaah, this is lovely. Lovely, lovely, lovely. I feel nice and cool again now' Mrs Poo said dreamily.

'It's just like being on a cruise' said Mr Poo with a smile. 'A poo cruise!' They both laughed as they floated past little rocks and tall trees, looking up at the clear blue sky.

Chapter Poothree: Shrink

A mile or so further along the stream, Mr Poo was lovingly gazing at Mrs Poo when he suddenly stopped smiling. 'Erm, darling?'

'What it is my love?'

'Have you lost weight? I mean, you're still very pretty and everything, but you look like you're... shrinking!'

Mrs Poo looked down at her body. 'Oh no!' she screamed. She was indeed smaller than before, with a few small holes appearing in her little brown body.

She then stared in horror at her husband. 'You're shrinking too, look!' Mr Poo looked at his body and saw that now he also had a few holes.

They looked back and were shocked to see little bits of poo - little bit of themselves - floating behind them.

'Argh, it's the water, we're... we're falling apart!' Mr Poo gasped. He desperately looked around and noticed something sticking out from the side of the stream. 'Quick, swim to that bit of grass over there!' he shouted.

They swam and swam as hard as they could, which can be difficult when you're full of holes, until they finally climbed up out of the stream and onto the grass.

'Huh, well, at least we're still in one piece,' said Mr Poo, trying to cheer up his wife.

'Maybe, but now we're smaller... and full of holes!' she sobbed.

'Don't worry dear, look at that big poo over there!' He was pointing to a large brown mound lying on the grass nearby. There were flies buzzing around it. 'Perhaps if we ask him nicely, he can spare some bits of himself to, you know, stick onto us. We've got to fill these holes!'

So they squelched over to the big poo lying by the stream. It didn't move at all.

'Hello there,' they smiled.

The big poo didn't reply. They tried knocking some of the flies off it.

'Er, hello?'

The big poo still didn't say anything.

'Excuse me, we are talking to you!' snapped Mrs Poo.

'Erm, I think this poo might be, um, a bit dead' Mr Poo said in a sad voice, giving it a little nudge with his leg.

'Dead? Really? Oh. How sad. Hum. Well, do you think he'd mind if we, er, borrowed a few bits then? I mean, he doesn't need them anymore, does he?'

So they took a few pieces of poo from the big dead poo and started sticking it onto themselves, until there were no more holes.

'Ah, that's better. Back to normal again' grinned Mr Poo.

Chapter Poour: Park

The Poos then walked up a little hill next to the stream and found themselves standing in a small park. 'Wow! So much space to run around in' squealed Mrs Poo in delight. 'Chase me!'

Mr Poo went squelching off after his wife, giggling like a little boy. 'Come here, I'm going to give you a great big pooey kiss!'

But just as he was about to kiss her, they both heard a loud barking noise coming their way.

'Hooray, it's a dog! Let's see if we can hide inside its bottom!'

'Good thinking. I'll call it over' Mr Poo said. 'Hello! Doggy!'

The dog ran over to them, but it was being followed by its two-legged monster.

The Poos froze...

The dog sniffed at Mrs Poo, then Mr Poo, then at Mrs Poo again. Next it stuck out its tongue and gave her a lick!

'Ooh, hi hi, it tickles' she giggled quietly, until the dog then opened its mouth and nibbled at her.

'Ouch!' she cried, trying to keep still and not make too much noise.

'Yuck! Stop it!' yelled the owner, pulling the dog away. 'Don't be so disgusting!'

'Phew, that was *horrible.* I wanted to climb into its bottom, not into its mouth! I think I really, really, *really* don't like being outside.'

'Me too! Why couldn't someone just put us in a nice big bag, like that lucky poo we saw earlier?'

'Yeah, being in a bag looks much safer, and it has to be easier than trying to jump up into a dog's bottom. It's just not fair!' Mrs Poo started to cry.

Chapter Pooive: Bicycle

Dring. Dring dring. There was another noise. 'Uh oh, what now?' Mr Poo asked himself.

All of a sudden a monster came riding up towards them on two big wheels, ringing a bell. It was moving very quickly.

Dring. Dring dring. The ringing got louder.

By the time the Poos knew what was happening, it was too late. There was no way to escape.

The wheels rolled right over Mrs Poo, squashing her flat in the middle.

A piece of her stuck onto the back wheel and off it went with the bicycle, spinning round and round. *Dring. Dring dring.* The ringing grew quieter.

'Noooo!' Mr Poo yelled out, running over to his wife. He tried picking her up, but her middle part was now stuck into the grass.

'It's too late for me, my love' she moaned. 'Save yourself, get out of here...'

'I'm not going anywhere without you!' Brown tears began falling from Mr Poo's sad poo eyes.

Very carefully, he managed to lift Mrs Poo up without her breaking in two. 'Ooooh' she groaned.

Next, he started to gently roll her back and forth on the grass, trying to help her get back to being a lovely sausage shape again.

Back and forth, back and forth he rolled her, like she was a lump of smelly brown putty, until her middle part had been evened out.

Finally, Mrs Poo could stand up again. 'I love you!' she said as she gave her husband a great big squelchy kiss. The Poos held each other close and cried.

Just then, they heard the monster of the dog that had nibbled Mrs Poo returning. The Poos froze once more, holding on to each other tightly.

'I guess I'd better pick this mess up in case someone steps in it, it's dangerous eh' it said to itself as it bent down towards the Poos with a plastic bag in its hand.

Mr and Mrs Poo smiled at each other as they were put into the bag together and then carried off to the nearest dog poo bin.

Safe, comfortable, and cuddling again...

Follow-up questions...

How can you tell that Mr & Mrs Poo love each other?

What would you do if you saw them on the pavement in front of you?

Have you ever known a dog (or any other animal) to eat a poo before? I wish I didn't!

Why do you think the dog owner finally picked them up and put them in a dog poo bin?

What other dangers do you think the Poos might have faced? Can you think of a new scene and make a drawing of it?

Stanley and the Poo Monster

Chapter One: Sad

Stanley Stevens was very sad.

He was already nine years old but still only looked about seven. Skinny with plain brown, unbrushably thick hair, he was a 'nice but quiet' boy, as his teachers always wrote in his reports.

He didn't know if he was good or not, but he always tried to be nice anyway, even though his classmates weren't. Maybe that is why he was usually quiet.

Every day at school, his classmates teased him.

When he first joined his school he felt very nervous, and on his very first day there he accidentally made a noisy smell. He only did it once, but everyone noticed, then everyone laughed. They laughed a lot.

So from that day on, whenever anybody made a smell, they would always say, 'Phwoar, who dunnit? It was smelly Stanley Stevens again! Hahaha!'

'But it wasn't me!' Stanley would cry.

Yet they just laughed even more. His classmates never seemed to become bored of the same old boring joke.

Stanley sometimes tried to tell his parents about it. But they did not listen. They always appeared to be much more interested in whatever was on the television than anything Stanley had to say.

'People at school say I smell' he'd complain.

'Oh, never mind dear,' they would say, not even looking away from the TV. If he tried standing in front of it to get their attention, they would just tell him to move. 'You're in the way Stanley, we can't *see!*' After a while he gave up. Even when it was dinner time, they would still just sit and watch the TV, chewing away like cows, Stanley thought, cows with square eyes. In fact they both looked a lot like Stanley, and each other! Pale, thin, messy hair and quite, quite miserable – unless the TV was on.

To make things even worse, Stanley's big sister would tease him too.

Tilly was double Stanley's size, with even messier hair, and was the complete opposite of 'nice but quiet.'

'Hey Stanley, where's your teddy hiding?' she would often ask him with a sneer. 'Maybe he's in the rubbish bin again, or the toilet bowl? Hahaha!' This was a favourite hobby of Tilly's, hiding Stanley's teddy bear, called Teddy, in various disgusting horrible places.

Stanley would try to tell his parents about his big sister, too.

'Mum, dad, Tilly's hidden Teddy again!'

'Oh, never mind dear,' they would say, again not looking up from the TV. Sometimes he wondered if they even knew he was there.

The one thing that made Stanley happy was playing with his pet dog Snaffles and his hamster, Hammy. They seemed to like him too. They were his only friends.

He liked to think at least *they* listened to him. But they could not talk, so how could he know?

Despite having Snaffles and Hammy, he was always miserable at school and nearly always miserable at home.

One afternoon, after being teased all day at school, and on his way to being teased and ignored all evening at home, Stanley didn't want to carry on walking. He stopped at an empty part of the street between his school and his house, sat down under a tree and began to cry.

'Why do people have to tease me?' he sobbed. 'What did I do to them?'

Suddenly he heard footsteps, they were coming closer. He wiped his nose, rubbed his eyes and was about to stand up when a strange looking shadow appeared before him.

He had seen that shape somewhere before. 'Wow' he whispered.

Chapter Two: Juice

Stanley slowly looked up. The shadow belonged to a little old man. The other children called him 'Willy the Weird Wizard' - but he'd never really spoken to him before. He used to be the science teacher at Stanley's school. Tilly said he was funny, for a teacher, but the school finally make him retire because he was too old.

Willy was wearing an unusual hat and cloak and had a big bushy beard. There was so much beard that Stanley could hardly see his wrinkly old face.

'Whatever's the matter young Stanley?' Willy asked kindly.

'Everyone always teases me. My classmates tease me at school, my sister teases me at home, and my mum and dad just ignore me and watch TV' Stanley muttered, trying hard not to start crying again.

'Ah, I see. Well, that *is* a pity.' He scratched his beard and Stanley honestly thought he saw something drop out of it - it looked a bit like a cornflake.

'Yes, I remember your sister. Tilly isn't it? *Poor you -* that's all I have to say about her.'

He rubbed his beard again and another cornflake fell out of it onto the ground. Stanley wondered if that's where he kept his snacks, in case he ever became hungry.

'Hmm, well, I wonder... I may have something that can help you, young master Stanley.'

'You do? What is it?'

'Here.' There was a clanking sound as he reached inside his cloak and carefully pulled out a pair of little bottles. One red, one green. They had liquid in them.

'This, master Stanley, is the last bottle of my special homemade anti-teasing juice' Willy said proudly.

'Huh? Your anti-whating what?'

'Haha, *anti-teasing juice!*'

Stanley didn't know what to say. He wasn't really sure what the old man was talking about but didn't want to risk asking any stupid questions.

'But Stanley,' Willy went on, 'just promise me you will be careful with it, alright? It can be rather dangerous.' He hesitated, then handed the two little glass bottles over to him, their red and green liquids swilling about inside. They looked fizzy. 'Just one gulp should be more than enough.'

'But there are two bottles, Mr. Willy.'

'Yes, you may well need that green one too. Like I said, the juice can be dangerous' Willy pointed a bony little finger at the red bottle. 'Well, too dangerous for an old man like me now anyway. Ok, you go straight home Stanley, show these bottles to your parents, and ask their permission if they will let you take a little sip, just to see what happens. The juice can affect different people in different ways – it really just depends on what you need it for...'

Chapter Three: Big

Stanley thanked Willy, said goodbye and took the bottles home. He was feeling quite confused, but a bit less miserable too.

When he got to his house he walked straight to the TV room to ask his parents' permission. There they were, his dad clutching the remote control, his mum holding a cup of tea. Almost like statues.

'Mum? Dad?' They ignored him. Stanley sighed and raised his voice. 'Weird Wizard... Erm, I mean Mr Willy, Tilly's old science teacher, gave me these bottles. He says I can try a sip, if you say it's ok?'

Still they ignored him.

'He says it's anti-teasing juice or something...'

'Oh, that's nice dear,' they said, not even looking up from the TV.

'Ah well', Stanley mumbled as he walked out of the room, 'Does *that's nice* mean the same thing as ok? I guess it might be alright anyway?' He gave Snaffles a stroke and took the bottles upstairs. He was walking into to his room to say hello to Hammy when he heard a familiar horrible sound.

'*That you Stanley?*' his sister Tilly yelled as he walked past her bedroom. 'Can you guess where Teddy's hiding today? Hahaha!'

Stanley stopped and looked at the bottles, then at Tilly's room, then back at the bottles again. He had a little think to himself.

He quietly crept inside his bedroom, said hello to Hammy who gave him a little squeak back, sat on the bed and very carefully opened the red bottle. It smelled like rotten cabbage. 'Phew wee!' he said, holding his nose. 'Hey Stanley!' he heard Tilly scream. 'Don't try pretending you're not there! If you don't find Teddy in the next five minutes I'm going to flush him down the *toilet!*'

That was it. 'Anti-teasing juice eh?' he said to himself as he lifted the bottle to his lips and tilted his head back. It fizzed up his nose making him cough - and it tasted even worse than sprouts!

'*Blugh!*' He managed to gulp one whole disgusting mouthful down.

Straight away, Stanley started to feel quite different. *Twang!* The springs in his mattress began making a noise as he felt himself sinking into his bed. He quickly stood up and hit his head on the light hanging above him. 'Ouch!'

He then saw himself in the mirror by the bed. He *looked* different!

He was taller - his trousers now looked like shorts - and his muscles were so big they were ripping his clothes.

'Wow, nobody will want to tease me now!' His deep booming voice echoed around the room.

Hammy took one look at him and started squeaking with shock, so Stanley picked her up to give her a stroke - but almost crushed her, her eyes nearly popping out of her head!

He then tried putting the hamster down gently, but did it with such strength that she bounced and landed with a splat. Hammy gave one more frightened squeak and ran off into her cage, hiding under some cotton wool, shivering with fright.

Snaffles then ran into the room to see what all the fuss was about. As soon as he saw the giant Stanley he began barking wildly.

Stanley tried stroking him to calm him down, but did it with so much power that he just squashed him flat into the ground! Snaffles, whose legs were now sticking out in every direction, quickly got up again and ran out of the room with his tail between his legs, whining.

Chapter Four: Shaking

Stanley became afraid. He grabbed the green bottle with his huge fist and took a gulp. Thankfully, he could immediately feel himself returning to normal again, his huge muscley body shrinking back to a thin little figure almost immediately.

'Phew, wow, Willy was right, it really *is* dangerous!'

Stanley looked at the shivering ball of cotton wool in Hammy's cage, heard Snaffles whining downstairs, and had another think to himself. He walked over to the bathroom and lifted the toilet seat. There was Teddy, soaking wet. He took his poor wet teddy out of the toilet bowl and held up the red bottle. He looked one last time at the fizzy liquid inside and, with a sigh, poured it into the toilet. Steam rose from the water as he pushed the handle down, flushing it away. 'Sorry Willy' he muttered.

The next moment, Stanley heard a deep rumbling noise coming from somewhere behind the toilet.

Everything in the bathroom started shaking.

He threw Teddy into his room and ran downstairs to the living room where his parents were still sitting watching TV.

'Help!' he screamed. But they ignored him.

The rumbling grew louder.

'Help!' he shouted at them again. 'Huh?' his dad said without turning around, both of them still just sitting there staring at the screen.

Suddenly the whole house started to shake. So did the TV. Tilly ran screaming into the room.

Stanley's parents raised their eyebrows, opened their mouths, and finally turned around to look at him.

'Erm, I think there might be a monster in the toilet' he said, almost not believing it himself.

His parents' eyebrows raised even higher and their mouths opened even wider. They looked at each other and then started laughing at him. Stanley didn't know what else to say. He turned to Tilly who still looked very scared. Her face then turned white as a sheet as a huge roar came bellowing down from upstairs, followed by a great crashing sound.

'Argh! Monster!' she screamed. Stanley's parents jumped up quicker than he'd ever seen them move before and they all raced out of the house screaming at the tops of their voices.

Something followed after them, smashing the doorway into pieces on its way outside.

It really was a monster!

But it was brown, slimy, and it smelled bad. *Very* bad.

'Argh! Help! Poo monster!' they cried.

The monster - bigger than a car and stinkier than a sewer - squelched towards them.

They froze with fear right in the middle of the street. The monster opened its mouth and let out a terrible sound. *'ROAR!'* Bits of poo flew out of its mouth in all directions, hitting cars and trees.

Tilly was still screaming when a big chunk of poo hit her full in the face - some of it even went in her mouth with more landing in her big messy hair! She fainted on the spot.

Stanley's parents were now too afraid to even move. They just stood there staring at the monster in disbelief. It reached out a great pooey arm, which actually looked more like a tentacle, and grabbed them. The monster then lifted them up and opened its huge horrible mouth. They shouted to Stanley 'Run, run for your life!' but he was too busy looking for something on the floor.

'Got one!' he said as he picked up a large stone and threw it at the monster. Stanley couldn't throw very far, but the stone bounced along the ground and landed with a plop in the monster's leg. It let out a deafening roar and threw his parents high up into the air. They landed in a tree on the other side of the road, completely covered in poo.

They wiped their eyes and looked for Stanley. He was now standing in the middle of the street just hopping from side to side, not knowing where to try and hide from the terrible beast. 'Run! Ruurgh!' The smell was so bad that they started to vomit, while Stanley began running as fast as his thin little legs could carry him, back to the only place he could think of - his school.

The monster let out another tremendous roar and squelched off after him.

Chapter Five: Phwoar

Some of Stanley's classmates were still playing football in the playground when they heard him yelling.

'Phwoar, what's that smell?' they joked, 'it sounds like smelly Stanley Stevens. Hahaha!'

They looked up the street only to see something big and brown crashing down the road behind him.

'Argh! Monster!' they screamed as they ran inside the school while pushing each other out of the way. They were quickly followed by Stanley, with the poo monster close behind him.

It squeezed through the entrance and squelched its way up the corridor, grabbing at the terrified children and covering them with poo.

The teachers came running out of their classrooms to see what the all the noise was, and were instantly splattered with poo as well.

'ROAR!'

The Head Teacher came out of her office yelling 'Quick, everybody hide in the school hall *now!'*

But there was no escape. The monster squelched after them and into the hall.

'ROAR!' More poo rained down from out of its mouth, until the children and teachers had it all over their skin and clothes and were slipping about in it - some crying, some vomiting, some doing both. Even the Head Teacher now began blubbering like a baby!

The monster roared again and moved towards them, the ground shaking as it did, until they were all trapped in one corner, screaming louder than ever.

Stanley was just as scared as anybody else, but he realised what he had to do.

More frightened than he had ever been in his life, he started to slowly walk up to the monster. One of the teachers shouted 'Stanley Stevens, *no!*' But he tiptoed even closer to the fearful creature and its huge open mouth. The smell was so bad he nearly fell over.

The monster opened its great slimy mouth even wider as it came towards him, as if to eat him!

His hands shaking, Stanley felt for the little green bottle that was still in his pocket. He took it out and with all his strength threw it into the monster's mouth.

ROAR!

ROAR.

Roar.

Purr.

Squeak...

The monster was shrinking fast.

'Squeak, squeak.'

After only a few seconds, the terrifying monster had become just a small puddle of poo lying in the middle school hall.

Everybody cheered 'YEAH! OUR HERO!' and ran over to Stanley, hugging him and clapping.

'Phwoar! Get off me' he laughed, 'You're all so smelly!'

Stanley Stevens was very happy.

Follow-up questions...

If someone is teasing you, who do you tell?

Why do you think Willy told Stanley to ask for his parents' permission before he drank the juice?

If you were Stanley, would you have flushed the red bottle down the toilet like he did, or would you have kept it?

Do you think Stanley was right to save his horrible classmates?

What do you think the 'Poo Monster' looks like? Can you draw him in a scene from the story?

The Poo Princess

Chapter One: Hobby

A long, long time ago in a far away land, there was a little village. Around the little village were lots of little farms.

The people of the village were very hungry because the farms could not grow any food, and the farms could not grow any food because there was never enough rain.

On the littlest farm around the little village there lived a poor orphan girl. She thought she was a plain looking girl, neither too heavy nor too light, or too tall nor too short. Her hair and eyes were plain brown and her skin was plain too. She didn't think she was anything special at all, and nothing really special ever happened to her.

Her parents died when she was young, but she kept working on the little farm as she didn't know what else to do. Because she worked alone every day on her farm, feeling very unspecial, she didn't really have any friends either.

Nobody ever visited her. She lived in a simple hut next to her field full of dried up soil with a few rocks and patches of yellow grass. 'Why would anybody ever want to visit here anyway?' she sometimes asked herself.

In fact, the orphan girl was so poor and lonely that the only hobby she had was... pooing! Her favourite time was at the end of the day, when she would enjoy doing her evening poo after a hard day's work, just before going to bed.

One day, when busy digging away at the hard ground and feeling particularly tired and hungry, she looked up at the empty sky and cried out 'Where are you rain? Come on! *Where are you?'* and started waving her arms at the sun in anger. But she lost her balance, tripped and fell backwards, landing on something soft and squishy.

To her surprise, it shouted 'Get off me!'

'Woah! A talking snake?' she asked in disbelief.

The girl looked down and noticed a pair of pointy little green ears poking out from under her bottom. Attached to the ears was a little round green head, with a long pointy nose, big round eyes and chubby little cheeks.

'Urgh! What kind of snake are you?' she shrieked.

'I am no snake! I'm a gremlin, and now I'm a rather flat gremlin - so please get your big smelly bottom off me!'

'Big?'

'Oh. I mean your beautiful, lovely smelling bottom. But please stand up, I can't breathe' the gremlin coughed, 'quick... I'll do anything!'

But the girl was still too amazed to move. She could see his little green legs sticking out from the other side of her bottom, wriggling about and kicking at the air in desperation.

'Er...' she didn't know what to say. 'Alright, alright,' the gremlin cried out, 'I'll even grant you a wish if you'll just get off me right now. I'm begging you!'

Chapter Two: Hurry up

The girl had heard of gremlins before in tales the old people in the village used to tell, but she had never seen one for herself.

'Urgh' the gremlin gasped, 'Hurry up will you? Make your wish and get off me!'

But it was not so easy thinking of a wish with a gremlin squishing about, kicking and crying under her bottom. Her empty stomach rumbled loudly.

'Ah, I know! I wish that my field can grow food again!'

'Really?' asked the gremlin, sounding surprised. 'Difficult magic that is! You mean a poor girl like you doesn't want to be richer? I can easily do that' he coughed.

'No, no. I can't eat money, can I?' she replied.

'Ok, how about cleverer then? You don't seem too smart to me.'

'Maybe not' the girl snapped, 'but I know that being clever won't make it rain' and she pushed down on the gremlin with her bottom.

'Argh, alright, alright! Well how about *beautifuller?* A plain looking girl like you, don't you want that either?'

She pushed down as hard as she could.

'Huhuh, but that's what people usually ask for' he groaned.

'Maybe, but food doesn't grow on beautiful does it?'

Just thinking about food made her tummy rumble louder than ever.

'I'm so hungry! I just want to grow food as easy as...' she thought for a moment, 'as easy as *pooing!*'

'Hmmm. Very well, if you insist!' croaked the gremlin. She looked down at him again. She wasn't sure what gremlins were usually supposed to look like, but this one looked really rather grumpy.

'Now set me free before I'm flatter than a very flat thing!'

Chapter Three: Ouch!

Finally, the girl stood up. The gremlin was quite a fat little creature, though he actually did look a bit squashed in the middle - there were two dents in his belly from where her bottom had been sitting.

He took a deep, rasping breath and with surprising speed jumped up as quick as a flash, giving the girl quite a fright. He then hovered in front of her face and cackled 'Your wish is granted!' His breath smelt so bad that she nearly fell back onto her bottom again.

The next moment, in the blink of an eye he hopped like a frog high over the neighbouring farm and landed far away. With a few more bounces he was out of sight over the horizon, though she could still hear his cackling hanging in the air.

The girl couldn't really believe what had happened, but she started looking excitedly around her little field, hoping to see mountains of food growing all over the place. But there was none to be found.

'Oh no, he tricked me!' she cried. 'Never trust a gremlin!' She stomped back to her little hut, kicking a rock in anger and stubbing her toe. *'Ow!'*

She then went to the toilet to angrily finish her evening poo. She was sitting in there for quite a while but in the end it was such a tiny poo - it's hard to do a big poo when your belly has been empty all day. After that she went straight to bed, as usual, but was still very upset about the gremlin's trick...

'Maybe it was all just a dream' the girl wondered as she woke the next day. Her stomach rumbling already, she went to the bathroom to clean her teeth.

But as she opened the toilet door, something big and green and leafy hit her in the face, knocking her back onto her bottom. 'Ouch!' She gave it a rub and nervously tiptoed back toward the toilet. The door slowly creaked open to reveal an enormous plant full of juicy big tomatoes - and it was growing right out of the toilet bowl!

She rubbed her eyes. 'Well, I know I said *as easy as pooing*, but I didn't mean *this!*'

Chapter Four: More

From that moment on, whenever the girl could do a poo, she did it on a different part of her field - until it was soon full of great big plants growing all kinds of wonderful fruit and vegetables (the type of which often depending on which one she was thinking of at the time!).

There were strawberries, raspberries, blueberries, blackberries, mulberries, gooseberries and honeyberries. There was rhubarb everywhere, and in between the rhubarb there were peaches, apples, kiwis and grapes. She also had corn and cucumbers, eggplants and onions, watermelons, lemons and lettuce, peppers, peas and potatoes, tomatoes and beans. She even did a sprout poo once by mistake!

In fact, from almost every poo she did there quickly grew a different type of vegetable or fruit, all crammed into her little field until the farm walls were nearly bursting!

Everyone from the village and all around came to buy her food to eat. The people were so hungry that they even bought her sprouts - and *nobody* likes sprouts!

'Hmmm,' she thought, 'this is great. If everybody's so hungry, they will give me more money for my food. Soon I'll be as rich as a princess!' The girl smiled to herself as she started asking the poor villagers for more and more money. 'Why not?' she asked herself. 'Nobody ever helped me when I was hungry, so why should I help them now?'

A few weeks later, when sitting in her hut and laughing while she counted her piles of coins and filled her face full of delicious strawberries, the girl heard a horse clip-clopping towards her farm.

Curious, she stepped outside to see who it was, peering over her poo-plants.

'Wow! That's the handsomest man I've ever seen!' she squealed, her heart skipping a beat.

She could see that he wasn't too heavy nor too light, or too tall nor too short. He had a kind face with nice brown eyes and nice brown hair with nice plain skin too. She thought he looked quite special. But he did not seem very happy. Not very happy at all!

Chapter Five: Magic

'Excuse me, are you the farm girl who has been taking all the money from my people?'

'*Your* people?'

'Well, my father's actually. Hello, I am the King's son.' He climbed down from his beautiful white horse.

'Woah, a real prince!' Her face turned red. 'Oh, erm, well...' she mumbled, as she started feeling quite bad for having been so greedy.

The prince looked around her field full of food. 'How can you grow so much fruit and so many vegetables without any rain?' He looked at the girl more closely. 'Ha, maybe it's magic!' he joked, flashing a big friendly smile at her.

He then blushed. 'Ahem.' He cleared his throat, shook his head and became more serious again. 'Well, I'd really appreciate it if you could start asking the people for less money. Have you forgotten what it's like to be poor? To need help?' His handsome face became quite sad.

The girl began to feel very nervous indeed, and her stomach started to ache - she'd eaten way too many strawberries.

'Ah, I'm sorry' she said timidly, 'I really need to do a poo, right now!' and off she ran to the toilet.

'Oh, well, do you mind if my horse eats some of these apples while I wait?' the prince asked, but it was too late, the girl was already too busy pooing to answer him.

When she stepped out of the bathroom, the prince saw a giant new plant sprout right out of the toilet bowl just behind her. She looked at him and slammed the door shut.

'Wow, it *is* magic!' Shocked, he jumped on the horse and rode back to his castle as fast as it could carry him.

'It isn't! It isn't magic, I'm just lucky! Honest!' she called out after him, but he was already gone. She looked around her farm at all the lovely food and really felt quite guilty. She walked back inside her hut. Rich, healthy and feeling lonelier than ever.

Chapter Six: Pretty farm girl?

The next morning, when still in bed, the girl heard the clip clopping of a horse once again. 'The prince is back!' she shouted as she jumped up, dragged a brush through her hair, chewed some toothpaste and ran outside to greet him.

'I am sorry I left you so quickly yesterday,' he smiled, 'please accept this delicious drink as an apology. I told my mother that I had met a pretty farm girl,' he said, blushing and then looking at the floor, 'and she made it, just for you.'

'What pretty farm girl?' she shouted in a snap of jealousy, and then her face turned bright red. 'Oh, you mean *me?* Wow, thanks.'

The girl took the bottle and drank the whole thing in one go - it really was delicious. All of a sudden, her stomach started to ache - but it was too painful to run to the toilet this time!

The next moment, huge plants were growing up all around the girl, until soon she was completely hidden.

'Help!' she screamed. 'I'm stuck, and I can't stop pooing!'

Without stopping to think, the prince took out his sword and chopped his way through the thickening leaves and branches to where the girl was, fruit and vegetables falling down around him.

By the time he reached her, she was almost completely buried! He picked her up and lifted her with all his strength until finally she was standing above him, balancing herself on top of his shoulders. But still the pooing wouldn't stop and soon there were plants sprouting up on top of his head and all around him, too! More and more and more!

'Hold on to the nearest tall plant, I have an idea!' The girl hung on to a big corn plant that was growing up right next to her as the prince shook the vegetables and fruit off his head and shoulders and tried to climb up to where she was.

At last he reached her and without even thinking, he held her close and gave her a big kiss.

Her stomach ache, and also her pooing, suddenly stopped. So the plants stopped growing too.

They looked into each other's plain brown eyes and felt something very special.

'I am so sorry! It was all my mother's idea. I told her yesterday about seeing a plant growing from the toilet after you did your poo, and she made that strange drink for you.' He started to blush again. 'She said it would make you poo immediately, to see if what I told her was true. I really didn't mean to scare you!'

'But you saved my life!' she replied, tears rolling down her reddened cheeks. 'I promise that from now on, I will give my food away to anyone who needs it.' They hugged each other as they both slid down the corn plant and safely back onto the ground.

* * *

From that day on, there was enough food for all of the people, whenever anybody needed it. Everyone now loved the girl for her magic poo-plants as well as her kindness, and at last she felt quite special - as well as very lucky, too. She and the prince lived happily together for many years, with a toilet always full of plants!

What kind of story do you think this was (for example Romance, Drama, Comedy or Fairytale)?

If a gremlin granted you just one wish, what would you want it to be?

If a boy or a girl you really liked did a poo on your head, would you still try to save them?

Can you think of different ending to the story?

What do you think the gremlin looked like? How about the girl or the prince? Try drawing a picture of them in a scene from the story.

The Secret Adventures of Fartboy

Chapter One: Rumble

Little Stevie Size had a superpower.

He couldn't fly, he couldn't run fast, and he wasn't strong. In fact, he was quite weak - a thin pale boy who was much shorter than most children his age.

But it was his dream to be able to do something which others could not, and that dream was to become a master of farting.

He could make a smell whenever he wanted, and when he did, it was a bad smell. A *very* bad smell. He didn't really need to eat anything special to be able to do it, or try too hard to squeeze anything out.

You might think that this is not such a great gift, or wonder why anybody would ever *need* to make a smell. But Stevie thought it was wonderful, and that farting could be a very useful power to have - depending on the kind of trouble he might find himself in.

He called his smells 'rumbles,' because when he first discovered his superpower, his bottom made a strange rumbling sound whenever he did one. But since then he had tried to learn how to control the noises he made, sometimes releasing a silent but deadly ('S.B.D.'), or making a very loud noise like a machine gun just to make himself laugh or if had to scare away a stray dog or something.

Nobody else seemed to have such control over their own smells - in fact most people tried to never make a smell, or they always kept it a secret even if they did. He was always surprised how much people didn't like his own 'rumbles' - he honestly thought they smelled quite nice.

As proud as he was of his smelly skills, Stevie soon learned not to let anyone else to know about his secret superpower. He was afraid that if everybody knew, they would then blame him every time someone else let one rip. He was quite disappointed that he had to hide his gift from the world.

Chapter Two: Drop One

'Fartboy' Stevie secretly called himself. Sometimes, when his parents were out, he would draw a large 'F' on the front of his pyjamas and wear a sheet around his shoulders like Superman's cape, flying around the house by using his jet-butt and fighting imaginary criminals with his amazing bottom smells.

His biggest dream was to do this in real life. Stevie wanted to be able to use his clever little bottom to fire a smell in any direction – and at almost any distance – he liked. He tried practising his smell-making skills whenever he was alone, which meant his bedroom eventually smelled so bad that nobody ever went in there, not even his pet dog!

He sometimes tried to shoot a smell straight up someone's nose, or drop one right next to them and just leave it hanging there. He even tried blasting smells all the way to the other side of the house, and sometimes succeeded if he really tried.

When it worked, if he made his dad spit out his dinner (leaving Stevie to eat the rest), or his mum run out of the living room (so that Stevie could watch whatever he wanted on TV), he would feel like a real superhero.

However, his smells did not usually happen the way he planned. Often they made his parents angry, shouting 'Stevie is that you again? That's disgusting!' and sending him to his stinky little room. After a while he had to stop using his special fart-power altogether. This made him very sad.

Then one day at school, Stevie found he needed to use his rumbling powers for the first time in ages and more than ever before. It was a day that he would never forget...

Chapter Three: Blurt

It all started as the bell rang out for morning break.

Stevie and his classmates were running to the playground after a boring Maths lesson, when he heard his mean old teacher Mrs Miggins angrily yelling 'Playtime is cancelled! You all have to stay in class to finish your sums!'

'But Mrs Miggins, that's not fair!' they complained. But it was no use.

'Stop your whining and get back into class now, you horrible bunch of little blurts!' She often called the children blurts, though they didn't really know what it meant.

Mrs Miggins didn't just act mean, she looked mean too. She wore big pointy glasses and shoes, had a big pointy nose, in fact everything about her was big and pointy, thought Stevie, even her mouth!

So back to the classroom they went. Stevie sat down with a thump - he'd been looking forward to playtime all morning, so now he wasn't happy. He wasn't happy at all. Then he had an idea and put up his hand. 'Mrs

Miggins, what if we promise to finish the sums for homework? Will you let us play then?'

'Yes, can you? *Please?'* pleaded Sarah Smith who was sitting next to Stevie at the back of the class. He blushed a little – Stevie thought she was the prettiest girl in the school.

'I don't believe you!' Mrs Miggins snapped. 'It's wintertime anyway, what do you want to play in the cold for? Now just be quiet and do your work!'

Chapter Four: S.B.D.

'Hmm, what would Fartboy do?' Stevie asked himself. He imagined doing a deadly fart and shooting it like an arrow down the aisle straight into Mrs Miggins's face, knocking her right off her chair. The whole class would cheer him and could then spend the rest of the day playing outside, even if it was wintertime!

'Alright then, let's see what you can do' he whispered to himself, a nervous smile growing across his cheeky little face. 'You'd better get ready for a rumble, Mrs Miggins...'

On purpose, Stevie dropped his pencil on the floor behind him. He then got up off his chair, bent down to pick it up, pointed his bottom at his teacher, and tried to fire a silent but deadly right at her.

He managed to do it without making any noise, but as the S.B.D. wafted its way across the classroom, Stevie could see it was beginning to spread out too far, as some of the other children started to gasp and choke, looking at each other – and then at Stevie - suspiciously.

He was getting worried, maybe the S.B.D. was too big or was going in the wrong direction? More and more children started turning around to see where the horrible stink had come from. He could feel his face turning red – could it be that he had lost his amazing powers?

Suddenly, Mrs Miggins sat up straight, frozen stiff.

Her eyes widened and then slowly narrowed. To Stevie's great relief, he noticed her begin shuffling about in her seat while her face became a funny colour.

'Ahem. Er. Ah. Urgh' she mumbled. The children turned to face her again. Stevie grinned.

'It's alright children' Mrs Miggins coughed, 'I've changed my mind. Out, *out!*'

Stevie's classmates cheered and scrambled for the door, trying to hold their breath on the way out, while Mrs Miggins pushed her way through them with a tissue over her big pointy nose.

'Phew wee!' squealed Abbey Ahmed, 'smells like old Mrs Miggins has been eating rotten cabbage for breakfast again!' The other children fell about laughing as they ran out to play, Stevie with them. 'Fartboy's back!' he beamed.

Chapter Five: Botty Burp

Forgetting his coat, Stevie raced out onto the playground looking for his best friend, Colin Cooper, to play with. He was nearly as little as Stevie, with a voice almost as squeaky as a mouse, and was always fun to hang around with.

'Oof, argh, please, leave me alone, ouch' he heard Colin cry. Stevie followed the sound to the corner of the playground where the swings were and saw Big Paul Powers and Barry Barnes, the class bullies, taking turns pushing Colin into each other. They were double Colin's size, mean and scruffy looking.

It was like they were playing a game of catch, but using a child instead of a ball!

Stevie was quite scared of Big Paul and Barry, as any little boy would be. He wished he could use his bottom as a flame thrower and burn the hair right off their heads with a great fiery fart. He would be the hero of the school - perhaps the army would even give him a job if he could do that for real!

'Ow, argh, oof!' Poor Colin was near to tears. Stevie was afraid of the bullies but felt sorry for Colin, too, so took a deep breath and quietly crept up to them anyway, until he was crouching down just behind Barry.

They didn't seem to notice Stevie at all - they were too busy pushing poor Colin about. He could smell something strange and quite horrible. The closer he got to Barry, the stronger the stench became. 'Wow, he smells bad enough already!' Stevie thought, but he was planning to make him smell worse anyway...

'Rumble time' he whispered as he nervously squeezed out a hot, poisonous smelling botty burp. Stevie was so nervous, he did it too strongly and made a little squeaking sound with his bottom. He quickly ran away hoping the other boys hadn't noticed, leaving his smell behind him.

Barry soon stepped backwards into the botty burp. 'Urgh! What's that smell?' he croaked. He shoved Colin out of the way and looked at Big Paul who said 'What smell? What you on about?' But just then it reached him, too. 'Blurgh... Colin stinks! Run!' The bullies ran away in a mad panic, leaving Colin to wander off in the other direction, feeling quite confused but rather relieved too.

Chapter Six: Trouser Cough

After saving Colin, Stevie was about to go in and get his coat when he thought to himself 'Maybe I could do a nice hot smell to keep me warm instead?' He stopped by the swings and began daydreaming about making a smell so big and nice and warm that the whole playground became like a sunny beach...

Everyone was walking around the playground in their swimsuits, thanking him for making it so nice and warm. There was even a barbeque with music and dancing. Then old Mrs Miggins appeared - she wearing a bikini! The thought of that soon snapped him out of his dream.

He shivered as he remembered where he was, and was about to try dropping a big warm one when Mrs Miggins walked right past him. 'Um, maybe not!' he thought. So he went back inside to get his coat instead.

As he neared the classroom he heard a noise. 'Mmm, yummy!' Stevie peaked around the corner of the corridor. It was Harry Hobbs, filling his greedy face full of chocolate cake right next to where Stevie's coat was hanging.

'Hi Harry, erm, can I have some too, please?' Stevie asked politely. 'Get lost little Stevie!' Harry snarled. 'It's *my* birthday cake - and nobody else is allowed to have any!'

'Oh, ok then,' Stevie said, feeling quite upset. Leaving his coat, he started to walk away and muttered 'Prepare to be rumbled.'

'You what?' Harry spat after him, but Stevie had already disappeared back around the corner.

After a few more steps, he stopped and waited for a moment, listening to Harry munching away like a hungry hippo. He thought how cool it would be to let one go right on the cake when Harry wasn't looking. When he took his next bite, the chocolate would taste like poo and he'd start vomiting all over it. Stevie would then jump out and say 'I don't want your pooey cake anymore anyway!'

He smiled to himself as he imagined what Harry's reaction might be and then decided to try it for real. He had already used his superpowers twice that day, 'Why not?' he thought. Keeping as quiet as possible, he began straining his stomach. His face turned a shade of red as he tried to bend a nasty trouser cough right around the corner.

To his delight, Stevie heard Harry stop chewing and start sniffing. 'Eurgh, this chocolate bit tastes like poo' he groaned, 'I think I'm going to be sick!' He dropped his spoon on the floor as he ran to the toilet with his hand over his mouth.

'Wow, I'm getting better at this, Fartboy strikes again!' Stevie said as he went back and grabbed a piece of cake for himself. 'Mmm, yummy, very chocolaty... and not like poo at all!'

Chapter Seven: Trump

The bell soon sounded the end of morning break and after a couple of dull lessons later, in which Stevie spent most of his time fantasising about the next amazing adventures of Fartboy, it was finally time for lunch. As he sat down in the canteen to eat his school dinner – which he thought was what Harry's vomit might have looked like – somebody pushed him hard from behind.

'Hey *little* Stevie, I bet I can *easily* beat you at arm-wrestling' Big Paul Powers boasted. Barry Barnes was standing next to him, giggling.

'Oh, er, no thanks Paul, I just want to eat this dog food and go out to play' Stevie joked, trying to be friendly.

Big Paul gave him another shove. 'Hey, it's *Big* Paul to you, and I'm going to *beat* you. Now, let's do it.' He plonked his big body down next to Stevie.

'Hey look everyone,' Barry called out, 'Stevie thinks he can beat Big Paul at arm wrestling!' The other kids sitting nearby circled the table excitedly. 'You ready, weed?' Big Paul said menacingly, glaring right at Stevie as he gripped his hand and squeezed it tight.

Stevie froze, everybody was now watching and shouting. His hand hurt but he tried to hide the pain. Big Paul started counting down, 'Three... Two...' Stevie panicked, his body felt like it was turning to jelly. 'What would Fartboy do?' he thought. The idea came to him in a flash - he lifted his bottom just an inch off his seat and quickly forced out a smell, bouncing the trump off the chair and right up into his opponent's face.

Big Paul shut his mouth and screwed his eyes up. It looked like he was trying really hard, but his arm became as floppy as a sleepy snake.

'Three' said Barry. Crash! Stevie pushed Big Paul's chunky arm down into a bowl of yucky soup, splashing him in the face as it landed.

'Hooray!' Colin and the other children cheered, patting Stevie on the back as the bully stood up slowly, looking quite ill. 'You've been rumbled' Stevie chuckled with relief as he watched him stagger back to his own table, the foul rumble still stuck up his nose. He was beginning to feel like a real superhero now...

Chapter Eight: Stink Bomb

After finishing their disgusting school lunch Stevie ran outside with Colin onto the playground. They played a game called *Knights and Dragons* with two other friends, Ibrahim and Nigel. He and Colin were the knights and Ibrahim and Nigel were the dragons.

The dragons were chasing after the knights and trying to eat them, while the knights used their swords (little sticks) to defend themselves and help each other. Stevie got caught and eaten first and had to sit down while he watched the two dragons chasing Colin the knight all around the playground. He imagined what he would do if the school was attacked by real dragons.

As big as airplanes and with teeth as sharp as steak knives, they swooped down on the school, breathing their flames onto the playground. They melted the swings, burning Big Paul Powers and Barry Barnes into little pieces of coal.

Then Mrs Miggins ran outside to shout at the dragons. They flapped their great scaly wings and swooped down again, one of them gobbling her up into its huge mouth. 'Urgh, yuck!' it roared, spitting her out.

She landed with a big splat in the middle of the playground, bits of her splattering all over the floor and walls.

Finally Fartboy stepped out dressed in his superhero costume. 'Yes, Fartboy is here!' Colin shouted. 'Save us Fartboy!' Sarah Smith cried out. He used his jet-butt to fart his way high up into the air. The dragons flew after him, roaring loudly and breathing their fire, burning Fartboy's cape.

He was weaving his way in between the flames and their huge swishing tails when he suddenly stopped and turned to face them. 'Go back to wherever you came from!' he bellowed. 'No Fartboy, it's too dangerous!' Sarah Smith called out to him.

The dragons roared even louder and just as the terrifying beasts were about to eat him, he bent over in mid-air and fired a stink bomb right into each of their wide open mouths. They started to cough, smoke coming out of their ears, and fell crashing down to the ground, landing on top of the school.

The school was destroyed and the dragons were dead. Stevie used his jet-butt to land safely in the middle of the playground as the whole school cheered his name. 'Fartboy! Fartboy!' Sarah Smith ran up to him and was giving him a big hug when he suddenly felt a large hand grab his shoulder.

Chapter Nine: Toot

He was being shaken out of his fantasy. It was Big Paul again.

'You think you can beat me, eh weed? Rematch, now!'

'Nah nah little Stevie Siiize is going to looose!' Barry Barnes sang and clapped around them. Stevie tried running away but they started to chase after him.

Big Paul began singing too. 'Nah, nah. Little Stuh, huh, argh. Eurgh!' He stopped running and put his hand over his nose. 'You let one rip Barry?'

Barry stopped too. 'What you talkin about? I can't smell anything - it must've been you!' Barry shouted angrily.

Stevie turned around. 'I can't smell anything either' he shouted at them, trying not to smile, but they were now too busy arguing to hear him.

'It *was* you!' Big Paul argued, 'That's why I lost at arm wrestling too. It's been you all day Barry - you stink!'

Thanks to the mysterious toot, it was like they had completely forgotten Stevie was there at all. He skipped away to the sound of Big Paul and Barry fighting behind him. 'Hehe, don't mess with the rumble master' he grinned. However, he wasn't even sure whether he had done the secret stink himself or if it was Barry Barnes all along...

Chapter Ten: Honk

Stevie then spotted Colin sitting alone by the swings. He'd been captured by the dragons too and now Ibrahim and Nigel had flown off to try and eat somebody else. 'Hey, Colin!' he called out and was about to walk over there when crazy Keisha King - another rather scary classmate of his - suddenly jumped out in front of him. 'Kiss me, Stevie Size!' she teased, while her friends nearby started laughing at him. Stevie froze with shock.

She moved towards him. He then saw Sarah Smith standing there, watching what was happening too. He suddenly panicked and cracked out a bum whisper right there and then. It was a bad one and it soon reached Keisha.

'Pooh, yuck! How can you stand that smell?' Keisha whined. But she didn't run away, and Sarah was still standing there watching him.

Scared and embarrassed, Stevie's bum honked again, this time quite loudly. He was losing control of his superpowers! Keisha's friends roared with laughter, but still she wouldn't go away! She just pinched her nose and walked up even closer to him, sticking her lips out and making a horrible kissing sound. The laughter grew louder and louder.

Stevie was too frightened to move – he could not even think what Fartboy would do – but he really didn't want to kiss Keisha King, especially not in front of Sarah Smith. 'Rumble attack!' he shouted in terror as he noisily broke wind, his whole body shaking as the rotten gas fired out of his bottom, nearly ripping a hole through his trousers.

The new smell hit Keisha who stopped, closed her eyes and fell to the ground. It soon reached her confused friends, whose laughter turned to screams as they went running for their lives.

Chapter Eleven: Stinker

"Wow, *cool!'* said Colin, who had been watching the whole thing too. 'How did you *do* that?' he asked admiringly, 'She's fainted and everything!'

Sarah Smith just stood there staring at him.

Suddenly he then heard an even more horrible noise than Stevie's foul butt blurts. 'You boy, stay there and don't move!' It was Mrs Miggins, who was pointing right at him with her mean pointy finger! She then came running over to where Stevie and Keisha were.

It was all turning into his worst nightmare. He panicked and slipped out yet another horrible stinker - this time completely by accident.

Mrs Miggins took one whiff, stopped still and fainted too!

'YES!' Colin roared. 'Hey everybody, look! Stevie's knocked crazy Keisha and Mrs Miggins out, just using his bottom!'

'No Colin! Don't tell anyone!' Stevie pleaded. But it was too late.

The whole class started running over to where they were and Stevie was just about to burst into tears when they suddenly began cheering and dancing with joy around Mrs Miggins.

Sarah Smith was cheering too as a huge smile lit up across Stevie's blushing face. Everyone appeared to know that it was him who had made the smell, but they actually seemed to *like* him for it. Was he *really* a hero? Should he just tell everyone about Fartboy? And maybe ask Sarah Smith to become Fartgirl?

But his moment of glory did not last long. As soon as Mrs Miggins started to wake up again they all ran away, laughing loudly. Were they laughing at him? Had he misunderstood? What if everyone knew his secret now? Mrs Miggins stood up and glared at him angrily. 'I'll get the blame for every smell ever from now on!' he worried.

Chapter Twelve: Stench

The next day, Stevie made quite a lot of extra pocket money. The rest of his class (except for Paul and Barry, who had been suspended for fighting together) was queuing up outside the boys' bathroom, each of them holding a pound coin, while he hid in a toilet cubicle, bottling his smells one by one.

'Hehe,' chuckled Colin as he handed over his pound in exchange for a bottle of *Stevie's Rotten Rumble Revenge*, 'I can't wait to empty this right under Big Paul's nasty big nose.'

'Haha, I'm going to be rich!' Stevie said excitedly as he pocketed the coin, proudly gazing at his collection of bottled stenches, all ready for sale. He then picked one up, opened it, held it to his nose and took a big, deep breath of his own bottom gas. 'You know what Colin?' he said, 'I honestly think it smells quite nice.' 'Ee-yuck!' Colin cried out, 'You're crazy!'

Stevie then remembered what Mrs Miggins had said to him after waking up on the playground the day before: 'Farts are just like children, Stevie Size... People only like their own!'

Follow-up questions...

If you could buy a bottle of _'Stevie's Rotten Rumble Revenge'_, what would you use it for?

Stevie's superpower is making smells. If you could have one superpower, what would it be?

If Stevie didn't have his superpower, how else do you think he could have solved his various problems that day?

Big Paul and Barry Barnes are bullies. Why do you think they like to pick on their classmates? Do you know anyone like that?

What do you imagine Mrs Miggins looks like? Can you draw her in a scene from the story?

Ghost Poo and the Haunted Toilet

Chapter One: Holiday

'Holidaaaaaaays!' John cheered with a stretch as he woke up on Saturday morning. It was the first day of the Christmas holidays, and his parents were taking him away somewhere.

He was mostly happy just because he hated school so much. His teachers were strict, the other kids were mean and he was starting to think the big metal fence around it was to keep him in, rather than keep intruders out. Just the thought of having two whole weeks without going to school made him feel in the holiday mood.

John had no idea what his parents were planning for their trip, which made things even more exciting. 'Just think Albert,' he said to his old pet spaniel lying on the floor next to his bed, 'This time tonight we might be in a different country, listening to a different language, eating different food and everything!'

He looked around his little bedroom, with its peeling wallpaper and worn old posters of his favourite Liverpool soccer players, and said 'I mean it might be Wales or Scotland again, but they're still foreign

countries aren't they?' Albert looked at him and yawned
- his smelly breath waking John up even more - licked
himself, then went back to sleep, his big floppy ears
covering his soft brown face.

John got up and went to pee. He remembered he
hadn't done a poo for a couple of days, but his stomach
didn't hurt so he wasn't too worried. 'It'll come,' he
thought.

After peeing - and managing not to splash the toilet
seat, something he considered a success - he squirted
some toothpaste into the air and tried catching it in his
mouth. He caught some but most of it just landed on his
pyjamas. He'd seen a boy do it in a movie once and
thought it was really cool, but the only result was that
most of his clothes now had toothpaste stains on them.

After brushing his teeth he tried to force a comb
through his thick, yellow hair. It didn't make it. 'Argh, I
hate my hair, it's like a flipping toilet brush' he groaned,
as he took his mum's plant spray from the window ledge
and sprayed some water onto his head. He liked to think
it would also help him grow taller, just like it did for
plants, but he was still quite short and very skinny for

his age. But at least the comb finally made it through his hair so he no longer looked like a mad junior scientist.

He went back into his bedroom. It smelt in there, usually of a combination of stale farts and bad breath, though he was never sure how much of it came from him or from Albert.

John threw on his only pair of jeans (he would sometimes walk around the house in his underwear waiting for them to be washed and dried, as he didn't like to wear anything else) and his favourite t-shirt (which he found more comfortable the longer he didn't wash it, so it had its fair share of toothpaste stains), then went downstairs for breakfast. Albert followed behind him, yawning.

'Morning mum' he said. His mother, short and thin like John but without the messy hair and the toothpaste stains, turned around.

'Well, well, good morning, not so grumpy today I see?' John was usually not a very cheerful person in the mornings. 'Could it have something to do with being on holiday?'

'Maybe' he replied with a big toothy grin, 'but that depends on where we're going.'

'You'll just have to wait and see then won't you' his mother smiled, lighting up her pasty thin face, as she went back to preparing the packed lunch for the journey. The jam and peanut butter sandwiches were for John. 'Nice one mum, who could ever not like jam and peanut butter sandwiches?' he said cheerfully, 'They'd have to be crazy!'

He ate his cereal and waited until his mother left the room, then took out a spoon and scooped a big lump of peanut butter straight out of the jar. Next, he dipped it into the jam jar and put the whole thing in his mouth. It took him a while to chew - it was like eating a ball of glue - but he then put another huge scoop of the stuff in his mouth.

Just then he heard his dad coming down the stairs. Unlike he and his mum, his dad was huge. John sent Albert out to greet him but he just nudged him out of the way as John desperately tried to swallow the lump of brown and red goo before he reached the kitchen. He saw his huge belly enter the door first.

Big, bald and grumpy. They were three words John could choose to describe his dad. But he could also say strong, funny and kind. It always depended on what mood his father was in at the time.

'Morning sunshine' he said as he ruffled John's hair then looked at his hand. John didn't speak - his mouth was almost glued shut by the peanut butter. 'What's this?' he asked, 'Toothpaste in that frizzy mop of yours? I can't believe you're eleven years old now and we still need to remind you to take a bath.' He wagged a big sausage-like finger at him. 'You're not stinking the car out with us all afternoon, covered in toothpaste and goodness knows what else!'

Chapter Two: Can we stop?

'Hurry up John or we'll go without you!' his mum yelled. He was always late, but his parents never seemed to get used to it. He was drying himself after his bath yet his dad was already sitting in the car. *Beep!* 'And make sure you go to the loo!'

'I already did!' called John. 'Number one or number two?' replied his mum. John thought for a moment. He was already in trouble for being late, so didn't want to spend yet more time trying to do a poo. 'Number two!' he answered. 'Are you sure?' his mum asked suspiciously. 'Ok then, get a move on!'

'Alright, alright, I'm coming now!' John shouted. 'Have a bath. Have a poo. Hurry up.' he said to himself, 'this is going to be a relaxing holiday, *not!*'

He finally ran out of their little house and jumped into the back seat of the car with his bag - nearly sitting on Albert's tail - and away they went.

They drove out of the town and were soon in the countryside, until they reached a road by the sea. At first John was excitedly looking around for clues as to where they might be going, but eventually he ended up just sitting there reading his soccer magazine. 'You'll feel sick if you read in the car' his mum warned. 'It's ok mum, I'm fine.'

But after a while he could feel the lump of peanut butter slowly rising up from his stomach - though he kept on reading because he'd found a story about his favourite player, Steven Gerrard. However, before long he began to feel the sickly taste of the peanut butter coming back into his mouth. He was starting to regret being so greedy at breakfast.

'Urgh. Dad, can we stop for a bit? I feel sick.'

'That's because you've been reading that flipping soccer rag isn't it! No, we won't stop until we get to the hotel.' His chubby cheeks turned an angry shade of red.

'It shouldn't be long now dear,' John's mum said softly. 'But if you're going to be sick, do it in this.' She turned around and passed a plastic bag to him. Albert looked at him and whined...

It was already turning black outside and they were still driving up the coast. John looked out of the window, the sky was full of dark grey swirls and there was even a bit of snow starting to fall. His mum kept looking at the map and muttering to his dad, whose face was becoming grumpier with every mile.

'Are we nearly there yet? Where are we going? Can you tell me now?'

'For the last time, *no!*' his dad snapped.

They were now on a road without any street lights, or buildings, or anything other sign of life as far as John could see. Just rows of shadows zooming by. He was feeling more and more sick.

'Um, seriously mum, I think I'm going to throw up.'

'We'll have to stop the car dear' his mum said.

'What? Here? In the middle of nowhere? It's freezing outside. Tut, it's his own fault for reading a stupid magazine!'

'But dear...'

'Oh alright! But if you're going to be sick do it quickly, we're running late thanks to you and your bath.'

'It's not my fault they're lost' John thought as he got out of the car. Albert got out too, sniffed the cold air, did a quick wee and climbed back inside.

It was so dark by now that John could hardly see where he was going. He went to the nearest tree, bent over and instantly threw up. It was horrible while it was happening - the peanut butter and jam tasted disgusting coming back the other way, some of it even went up his nose and got stuck there - but at least he felt better once it was all over.

Beep! 'Alright, alright, you grumpy old...' he mumbled as he got back into the car, clearing his nose into the snow along the way.

'Yuck, very charming. Feeling better now then?' his mum asked.

His dad turned the key, the engine made a whirring sound, but the car didn't start.

He tried again. And again. And again. He then hit the steering wheel. *Beep!*

'Well that's just brilliant!' John and his mum didn't dare say anything.

After about ten more minutes of trying, his dad said 'That's it, I give up, and I can't get any signal on the phone so we can't call for help either.' He hit the steering wheel again. *Beep!*

'But if we stay here all night we'll freeze dear.'

'I *know* that!' He looked out of the window and shook his head. 'I suppose I'll have to get out and take a look around. Did you bring your torch with you John?'

But John was no longer paying attention. He could see a little light in the distance. It was moving.

Chapter Three: Lock your doors

'Hey, what's that?' John asked.

'What's what dear? Oh, look love, there's a light over there!'

'A what? Oh yes, well done John. Is it from a house or something?'

'No, it's moving. And it looks like it's getting closer.'

'Closer?' His mum asked, a little worried.

'Maybe we can ask them where we are?'

'You'll do no such thing. What kind of a person goes walking around in the wild in the middle of the night anyway? Lock your doors' his dad said. They all pushed their buttons down.

Suddenly, the light disappeared. 'It's gone out now dad.'

'Well yes I can see that.' His voice became a whisper.

They waited for a moment.

Tap, tap, tap.

'AARGH!' they screamed. Albert barked.

They all turned around and looked through the back window. The light suddenly came back on to reveal an old lady's face right outside the car.

'AAARGH!'

Albert's bark turned into a whine.

She gave a toothless smile, deep wrinkles creasing all over her face.

'Can I help you?' she croaked.

'Erm,' John's dad opened his window a bit, 'Can you tell us where we are please?'

The old lady slowly walked around the car to his door, carrying her lamp with one hand and holding her pink bathrobe together with the other - something John felt grateful for.

'I heard beeping and thought I'd come outside to see who it was. Are you lost?'

'Um, well, yes, sort of. But the car won't start now anyway.' He shot John a grumpy look.

'Well, you're in luck. You can't stay in the car all night but I happen to have a hotel, just up the road here.'

'Really?' John's mum chimed, 'That's wonderful! Have you got any rooms free?'

'Oh yes, hehe, I always have rooms, especially for people who are lost. Follow me, follow me' and off she waddled.

Chapter Four: Welcome

'Well I suppose we can leave the car here, it's not like anyone can steal it now, is there? Come on, grab the bags' his dad said, sounding quite relieved.

They took their luggage out of the back and followed the old lady - who was already well ahead of them - down a path leading from the road. Even using John's torch it was difficult to see where they were all going, nearly tripping over a few times, but finally they made it up the pathway and through some trees to the hotel.

'Hotel? Looks more like an old hut to me' John's dad muttered to his mum. Even in the dark they could see it was a small house, with tiny windows and a tiny door. It seemed ancient. There was nothing else around except what looked like a little shed next to a small garden at the front of the building.

As they stepped inside John could see that it really was old, and it smelt like his Grandma's apartment too. 'Well, at least it's warm,' he thought.

The hallway was small and cramped and the furniture looked about as old as the lady herself. It was dimly lit but John could still see that nearly everything was covered in dust and cobwebs.

'Come in, come in, make yourselves at home.' The old lady waved them in.

She didn't look any younger in the light. John couldn't help but stare at her. She was short and rather round and her back was bent, making her look even shorter and rounder. Her hair was patchy and her nose took up about half of her face. He thought it was just a shadow before but it really was all just nose.

Albert let out a big yawn and sat down. The lady looked at him and said 'Pets are allowed but not in the rooms. Your dog can sleep here in the hallway if you don't mind.'

'That's fine' John's mum replied, looking at Albert and shaking her head. 'All he ever does is sleep and poop anyway.'

The old lady looked at her. 'Poop?' she said, her voice higher than before. He noticed she also had hair on her face. Not just a few wisps like most old people but patches of grey stubble everywhere. He felt slightly sick again.

'Oh, don't worry' John's mum said, 'he's house trained. We've got a cushion for him to sleep on too.'

She gave John a nudge and he took the cushion from Albert's bag and threw it into the corner. The dog slowly got up, walked across the hallway, sat down on the cushion with a yawn and fell asleep almost immediately.

'Ah, lovely. Well, my name is Mrs Barber, but you can call me Barbara.'

'Barbara Barber?' John grinned. His mum glared at him.

'Welcome to my hotel.' She held out her hands revealing dirty stains under her armpits. In fact, her entire bathrobe was covered in them - brown, orange, yellow - like a rainbow of dirt.

'Erm, right. Thanks.' His dad's face still looked quite grumpy. 'So how much for two rooms? Any chance of a discount? We'll be leaving early as we've got another hotel booked somewhere further along the coast you see.'

His mum coughed. 'Well, maybe we can stay for breakfast anyway.'

'Oh good, yes, we are famous for our breakfasts here at Hotel Barber' she smiled, her deep wrinkles and the gaps in her teeth increasing in number as she did.

They looked around the hallway again. 'Yeah right, maybe a hundred years ago' John mumbled to himself.

Chapter Five: Creaking

John's dad sorted out the payment as he and his mum creaked their way upstairs. 'The bathroom's first on the left if you need it' Mrs Barber called after them.

There was only one other floor, and it looked like it only had three bedrooms.

'Do you think she sleeps in that one then?' John asked his mum, nodding towards the door at the end of the corridor.

'I don't know, but I just hope the bedrooms are a bit nicer than downstairs' she said under her breath as she opened his door first. 'Well, at least you're right next to the bathroom.'

Having seen how old and dirty the hallway was, he was quite relieved. His room was small, with just a bed and a wardrobe, but it seemed ok.

His mum then opened his parents' room across the corridor. It was the same as his, only with a bigger bed.

'Hmm. It's a bit small, but it beats sleeping in the car hey?' she smiled at him. 'Now go and get ready for bed and use the toilet. Lights out in five minutes, I'm shattered.'

John changed into his pyjamas, toothpaste stains and all, and was about to go to the toilet to finally attempt to do a number two when he remembered he hadn't finished that story about Steven Gerrard. He sat on the bed and picked up his soccer magazine. Every time he moved, or even breathed, it creaked, as did the floorboards whenever he stepped on them, or the wardrobe whenever he opened it. 'It's like being on an old ship or something.'

There was a knock at the door. It was his mum and dad.

'Ok love we're off to bed now. Lights out ok?'

'Ok mum' he said, realising he still hadn't been for a poo.

'Sorry if I was a bit grumpy earlier. Mrs Barber doesn't have a phone,' his dad sighed, 'but she says there's a payphone about half a mile up the road. I'll call the car rescue people in the morning so hopefully we'll be at our hotel by lunchtime tomorrow.' He looked up and down the little corridor and whispered 'It should be nicer than this place anyway!'

John giggled as his mum jabbed her bony elbowed into his dad's big belly. 'Shush, she might hear!'

His dad just laughed. 'Alright then son, sleep well.'

'Ok, good night.'

He creaked back across the room and sat on his creaky bed again. He was already feeling sleepy. Being car sick seemed to have taken most of his energy. He turned off the bedside lamp, climbed under the covers and was asleep in no time.

Chapter Six: Noises

Parp!

Plop!

Paaarp!

Plop, plop.

John woke with a fright. 'Hello?' He looked around but it was too dark to see anything.

His stomach hurt.

Parp! Plop.

'URGH! Someone's pooing right next to my head!' He tried using his pillow to cover his ears, but it was no good.

It was so loud and clear, John felt like he could almost smell what was going on. But he really needed to go to the toilet! He hoped and prayed there was another bathroom in the hotel, as he certainly didn't want to follow whoever was in there right now.

The noises kept coming. 'Dad must have stomach ache too or something' he thought.

He got up, put on his dressing gown, opened his door as quietly as possible and tiptoed along the corridor to the bathroom.

'Dad?' he whispered.

Paarp! Plop!

'Dad?' he said again, a bit louder this time.

John then heard some of the worst pooing sounds he had ever known. His stomach turned. He desperately needed the toilet but he could even smell what was happening just from under the bathroom door. He gasped and held his nose. It was like a poisonous gas.

'Dad!' he called out, 'How long are you going to be in there?'

'Oh, quite a while' a voice said. But it wasn't his dad, it was the old lady!

'Oh, erm, sorry. Er, is there another toilet I can use please?'

The old lady grunted. It was terrible.

'Oh, well, there is, but it's outside. I don't think you'll want to go out there though dear, it hasn't been used for quite some time.'

More parping and plopping followed. He couldn't stand the noise, the smell or the pain in his stomach. He was starting to do the toilet dance just to hold it in.

'Ok, thank you.' He tiptoed back into his room to put his shoes on and get his torch.

'But I must warn you dear...' the old lady croaked, but it was too late, John was already halfway down the stairs.

There was a lamp on at the entrance so he could see alright, but it was still quite gloomy and the hallway looked even spookier than before. Albert woke up as he crept past him and got up off his cushion. John gave him a stroke. 'Why didn't I just go to the loo when mum told me?' he whispered. He opened the front door and an ice cold breeze hit him, turning his breath to steam.

He tied his dressing gown tight over his pyjamas, switched on his torch and stepped outside. The door closed after him with a click. He shone the light in every direction but could not see anything that might have a toilet in it. There was just the path, the small garden – which even just from the torchlight looked quite colourful – and the little garden shed, all surrounded by tall dark trees.

He looked back at the shed again. 'Oh, you've got to be joking.'

Chapter Seven: Come in

He walked hurriedly, a thin layer of fresh new snow quietly crunching under his feet, until he reached the door. But there wasn't a handle. He looked around the side too but there wasn't even a window for him to look into. He shone his torch at the door again. 'No handle?' He was getting desperate.

He tried pushing it but it didn't move. He pushed harder but still nothing. 'Oh come on!' He gave it a kick and stubbed his toe. 'Ouch! Open up you stupid door I need to poo right now!'

Just as he turned to go back inside the hotel, dreading using the stinky bathroom after Mrs Barber, he heard a creaking noise behind him.

It wasn't like any of the creaking he'd heard in the hotel. Maybe it was his tiredness, or his stomach ache, or his desperation to do a poo, but he honestly thought it sounded a bit like *coooooome iiiiiiin.*

He spun back around so fast he almost fell over. The door was opening inwards until the gap was wide enough for him to squeeze through, but he couldn't see a thing inside - it was pitch-black. He shone his torch through the gap.

There, at the back of the little shed, there was indeed a toilet. 'Phew.' As he slowly stepped inside he could see that the thing was about as old as the hotel itself. There was a toilet bowl with a big wooden seat. From it ran a rusty pipe leading up to a dirty metal box above the bowl, which had a handle hanging down from it on a chain.

'Some holiday this is. Thanks dad!' He walked towards the toilet.

There didn't appear to be anything else in the there, not even a basin to wash his hands in. But even just by using the torch he could see that the shed hadn't been cleaned for ages - it was possibly even dustier and had more cobwebs than the hotel hallway.

'Well at least it doesn't smell.' He went further inside.

BANG!

The door slammed shut behind him. He nearly pooped in his pants right there and then.

'Huhuh, it must be the wind or something.'

John paused for a moment and at last sat down on the cold toilet seat. 'Aaah' he groaned as he started to relax, until at last he finally heard some comforting plopping of his own. He balanced the torch on his lap while he rubbed his hands together to keep them warm.

Just as he'd finished doing his business and reached for some toilet paper, he came to realise there wasn't any to be found.

Chapter Eight: Don't flush

'Oh, that's just great!' He rummaged around in his dressing gown pockets and found a few old tissues. He might have already blown his nose on them but he had no choice. He wiped his bottom, pulled his pyjama trousers back up and reached for the handle.

His hand hit the chain and it clattered loudly against the metal box above his head.

'NOOOOO!'

'What the?' John jumped back so far he hit the shed door, dropping his torch.

'Pleeeeease, noooo! Don't flush!' said the voice, with a squeak more than a scream.

'Who's there?'He was shaking with fright.

'Who's where?' said the voice.

He was frantically feeling around for his torch on the cold, dirty floor.

'Who are you?'

'Who am I?' replied the voice.

Finally John felt his torch on the floor, picked it up and - hands trembling - switched it on.

He shone it all around but could not see anybody else.

'Where did you go?'

'Where did I go?' squeaked the voice. It sounded like it was coming from the toilet!

John turned and tried to open the door but there was no handle on the inside, either. He started to panic.

'Excuse me?' asked the voice.

He looked around at the toilet again and shone his torch on the bowl.

'Show yourself!' John said, though he wasn't sure he actually wanted to see who, or what, the voice was coming from.

His heart almost thumping out of his chest, he slowly walked up to the toilet. Trapped, terrified, but curious too.

He took a deep breath then shone his light into the bowl. He froze with shock.

There, floating above the toilet paper John had left in there, was a poo.

But it wasn't floating on the water, it was floating in the air, in the middle of the bowl!

And it was moving.

'Argh!' John cried out.

'Hello' it squeaked. John jumped back again but this time fell onto his bottom with a thump. He just about managed to keep the torch shining on the bowl. The poo slowly rose up out of it and floated towards him. John's hand was shaking so much that it was hard to keep his light fixed on the floating poo.

'What's your name?' it asked. As the poo spoke, a little hole opened up at one end - almost like it had a mouth.

'J-J-J-John.'

'Hello J-J-J-John. I'm happy to meet you.'

Chapter Nine: It's just my name

'Wh-wh-what are you?' he asked, not believing his eyes or his ears.

'What am I? Or who am I? Well, I suppose I'm what you might describe as a ghost poo. But you can call me Frank.'

'Frank?'

'It's just my name. You know, I've been alone in here a long, long time. Sometimes I talk to myself, so it's good that I have a name.'

'But, but what *are* you?'

'I just told you, I'm Frank.'

'You're Frank? The *poo?* The *ghost* poo?'

'Yes, J-J-J-John.'

'Oh, I'm just John.'

'Yes, just John.'

'No, I mean my name is John! This is impossible, how can a poo talk? And how come you're a ghost?' He felt ridiculous just asking such questions.

'Do you know how long I've been stuck in this toilet for, John?'

The poo floated a bit nearer, it really did have a sort of face, with little brown eyes and a little mouth. The torch light shone right through the poo and onto the wall without it even making a shadow. But John could still see it hanging there in mid air, right in front of him, like a kind of faded dirty brown sausage.

'Do you know who the last person that came in here to do a poo was?'

John didn't know what to say, but he couldn't stop staring at this thing floating before his eyes.

'It was me! Nobody else has sat on this toilet since that day, the day that hotel Barber was opened... Sixty years ago!'

'Wow, that's a long time,' said John, trying to steady his voice. He was still in shock, but found himself speaking anyway.

'You see, I had a terrible stomach ache that day' the poo said. 'And I had to use this old toilet, but I blocked it, just at the very moment that I died from the pain in my stomach. So I've been stuck in this horrible little shed ever since. It seems I can never leave.'

'Erm, ok.' John wondered if this was all some kind of a trick, but it felt too real.

'Er, why don't you just float out of the door then?'

'Ha, yes, that's what I'd like to know! It would appear, Mister John, that ghosts must stay in the place that their bodies die, that is if they don't make it to heaven or wherever it is everyone else goes to.'

'But how can a poo *die?* There's no such thing as a talking poo anyway!'

'Well, hum, maybe that's my punishment. I don't know if there's a heaven, but this is certainly my hell. I wasn't a poo when I died, Mister John. Oh no, I was not a poo at all. I was Frank Barber, Mrs Barber's husband.'

'Huh?' John finally stood up, keeping his torch light firmly pointed at Frank.

'It seems my spirit ended up passing into my poo, just as they both left my body at exactly the same time. So I ended up stuck all alone down this toilet bowl' he said, slowly drifting from side to side, 'and I've been here ever since.'

John shook his head, as if trying to wake himself from a nightmare.

'I suppose I'm lucky I wasn't vomiting instead!' Frank chuckled. But it didn't sound like a very happy chuckle at all. John remembered being sick earlier and shivered. He couldn't quite take it all in.

'Barbara's never used this toilet, though I like to think that's because she's always been too sad about my death. And none of the guests - if there ever are any - have been desperate enough to want to come in here either. That is, until tonight, John.'

Chapter Ten: Nice meeting you

'Wow.' John didn't know what else to say, or do.

Frank the ghost poo floated through the air right up to John's face. John couldn't smell anything but it was a horrible sight; a ghost poo with a man's face, talking to him, in a toilet, in the middle of the night!

'How is my wife anyway? Is she still beautiful? You know, she used to be the prettiest girl in the village... Oh how I'd *love* to see her again!' Frank looked like he was smiling, but it was hard to tell just by looking at his small poo-face.

'Er,' John wasn't quite sure what to say, 'Yes, yes, she's still, erm, beautiful, er, I mean pretty. I mean beautiful and pretty.' He wondered for a moment how Frank would feel if he saw Mrs Barber now with her stains and stubble. Then he wondered what she would think if she saw Frank the way he was now! John tried to put it out of his mind, the situation was terrible enough already.

'Well, it's been nice meeting you Frank, but I think I'd better be going back to bed now, it's quite cold. Erm, good luck with everything' John said nervously as he turned to face the door.

He shone his torch up and down it, but still couldn't see any sort of a handle. 'How do I open this thing anyway?'

'Ah, well, that's just it, you can't. Besides, do you really think I'd want you to leave?' The torch light caught Frank floating in-between John and the door. 'You're the first person I've spoken to for sixty years!' He began floating around John's head. 'Thank you for waking me up. Please, stay, be my guest' he squeaked.

'Erm, thanks, but that's ok, I think I'd better go now anyway.'

'But you *can't!'* Frank squeaked so loud it hurt John's ears as he zoomed faster and faster around his head.

'I have to!' shouted John. 'If I stay I'll freeze or starve or something!'

'So then you can stay here and haunt this toilet with me, perfect! At last I'll have somebody else to talk to.'

'No, I'm sorry but I'm leaving right now.' John ran at the door and kicked it with all his strength, which wasn't much, and fell back onto the floor again. The door didn't even move a millimetre.

The torch light started to fade.

'Oh no. No, no, no!' John fiddled with the switch, but the light soon flickered out.

'Welcome to hell, John' he heard Frank squeak, followed by horrible a cackle.

'Help! *Help me!'* John screamed.

'Nobody can hear you in here' Frank laughed. John could hear him still circling around his head.

'Oooh it's going to be so nice having a friend at last. Barbara never came, guests never came, but you came. Thank you John, *thank you!* Hihi!'

'Help! *Heeeelp!'*

Just as he was about to burst out crying, John heard another noise.

Woof! Woof, woof!

'Albert! *Albeeeert!'* John yelled.

'What's that? Your dog? It must have very big ears! But who's he going to tell?' Frank's squeaky voice echoed around the shed. 'Anyway, nobody can save you if you freeze to death before they find you in here. Haha!'

Chapter Eleven: Stuck

John started to cry. He couldn't see a thing, he was freezing cold, Frank's cackling kept whizzing around his head, and Albert had already stopped barking.

'Stuck in the toilet for sixty years alone, now it's *your* turn Mister John. Oh we'll be such good friends!'

'Stuck in the toilet' John sobbed, 'Stuck in the toilet.'

'Hihihihi.'

'Hang on a minute. Stuck. *Stuck* in the toilet. That's it!'

He got on his hands and knees and started feeling his way across the floor towards the toilet bowl.

'You can't escape. Why don't you just sit down and we can have a nice chat?'

John touched the bottom of the bowl with his hands and stood up, waving his arms in the air over his head.

'Wait, what are you doing?'

His hand hit against something hard and cold that made a jingling sound. He grabbed at the chain, caught it and quickly ran his fingers down it until they gripped around the handle.

'What are you doing John? Don't be so silly, wait, no, please, I just want to be friends. Don't do it!'

Flush!

It was too late. John was already pulling the chain down as hard as he could.

The toilet made the whoosh of a great waterfall as he heard Frank squeak *'Noooooo!'*

The squeaking faded, *'Noooo,'* quieter and quieter, *'nooo,'* until he could no longer hear anything from either Frank or the toilet, just silence.

He didn't know where Frank had gone to but he had no wish to stay and find out. Besides that, he was really starting to shiver from the cold.

He turned around and walked with his hands out in front of him until he reached the door. He pushed it as hard as he could but it was no use. He took a step back and tried smashing his shoulder into it, but it still didn't move at all. 'Ouch!' He gave his shoulder a rub. 'Oh come on, I need to get out of here right now!' he cried.

With that, the door started to open, slowly and loudly. To John's ears, the horrible creaking noise it made sounded a bit like *'goooood byyyye.'*

It soon opened wide enough for him to just about fit through. Leaving his torch behind on the floor, he squeezed through the gap and sprinted up to the hotel. The front door opened with a click and he stepped inside, slamming it shut behind him. Albert whined and hobbled up to John, sniffing him and licking at his hands.

'It's alright Albert, it's alright' he said, bending down to stroke him.

After a couple of minutes being comforted by Albert, he went upstairs and looked along the corridor. The hotel was completely quiet except for his dad's familiar snoring.

John didn't know what to do. Should he wake his parents and tell them what had happened? Should they get away from the hotel as soon as possible? But the car was broken down and there was nowhere else to go!

He suddenly felt a terrible tiredness come over him and let out a yawn even bigger than one of Albert's. He walked into his room and closed the door behind him. Kicking off his shoes, he threw his dressing gown onto the floor and collapsed on the bed.

'Where did Frank go to? Was he flushed down to hell or something? Are there other ghosts? Imagine being a poo stuck in a toilet for sixty years!' These thoughts and more were swimming around in John's head. It all was too much and he soon fell into a deep, long sleep.

Chapter Twelve: It's funny you should ask

There was a knock at the door.

'John?'

It was his mum.

'John wake up, you've already missed breakfast.'

'Mum?'

She popped her head inside the door. 'Get dressed and grab your things, you're dad's managed to get the car working again, we're leaving in a minute.'

'Great!' said John, jumping out of bed and quickly getting changed.

'Wow' said his mum, 'slept well then?'

'Er, no, not exactly. I don't know, not really.' He gave her a confused look. 'Anyway, I'm just happy we're leaving!'

'Oh, ok, well, see you downstairs in a minute then. And don't forget to go to the loo.' The door closed with a creak after her.

John sat down on his bed and looked around the room. Had it all just been a nightmare? It still felt real, but how could it be?

Then he saw it, still lying in his bag just like he'd left it the night before when he went to bed. It was his torch. 'Phew! Man, dreams can spooky!' he said to himself as he packed the rest of his things away.

He felt like he needed to go to the toilet, but took one look at the bathroom door and decided to definitely wait until they reached the next hotel.

His mum and dad were already sitting in the car when he ran outside carrying his things. Albert stuck his head out of the back window and greeted John with a bark.

'Ah, goodbye then' he heard Mrs Barber say cheerfully as she walked towards the hotel from the garden shed, giving John a bit of a fright. She looked different now. Still very old, but much smarter in her gardening clothes.

'Oh, goodbye Mrs Barber.'

He walked over to the car and threw his stuff onto the back seat next to Albert. 'Morning sunshine' his dad said. 'Hi dad.'

John stopped and turned around, looking at the shed. He felt a cold shiver run through his body. 'Can you hold on just for a second, I think I should go and thank Mrs Barber.'

'Oh, ok, if you like, good lad. But hurry up, we're running late again eh.'

John walked over to the colourful little garden where Mrs Barber was standing.

'Mrs Barber?'

'Yes dear?'

'Can I ask what you've got in that shed?' He pointed towards it without looking at it.

'Oh,' she said, 'just some gardening tools and the barbeque - though it's a bit too cold for that at the moment isn't it!' she joked.

'Hehe, yes, it is. Ok thanks, I was just curious. I thought it might be a toilet or something.'

'A toilet? Oh no dear, I don't think anybody would ever want to go to the toilet in a shed like that.'

'Sure,' John chuckled. 'Well, thank you for having us' he said as he went and got into the car, opening his window to wave goodbye.

'You know, it's funny you should ask about that shed' Mrs Barber called out after him. 'My husband Frank built it just before he died!'

'What?' John shouted as his dad drove the car down the path, while Mrs Barber smiled and waved them goodbye...

After his problems with feeling sick and needing the toilet, do you think John will listen to his mother more in the future? Why / Why not?

What kind of character do you think Mrs Barber was? Can you draw a picture of her?

If you were John, would you have: A) gone to the outside toilet, B) waited for the old lady to finish in the bathroom, or C) tried another way of doing your poo? Why?

What do you think Frank looked like? Can you draw him inside the haunted toilet?

How do you think John felt at the very end of the story? Can you think of a different ending?

'The Smell of Poo' bonus 'Pooems'

Pooem 1: 'Your Poo & You'

Big poos, small poos,
Dry ones, wet ones,
Poos that can float, poos that sink,
Ones that don't smell, ones that stink.

Neat poos, messy poos,
Ugly ones, cute ones,
Poos that are smooth, poos that are lumpy,
Ones that are long, ones that are stumpy.

Light poos, heavy poos,
Weird ones, tricky ones,
Poos that are quiet, poos that go plop,
Ones that won't start, ones you can't stop.

Happy poos, sad poos,
Flushing ones, stuck ones,
Poos that are wide, poos that are narrow,
Ones that go fast, ones that go slow.

Painful poos, easy poos,

Nice ones, nasty ones,

Poos that are curly, poos that are straight,

Ones you do early, ones you do late.

Healthy poos, sick poos,

Even ones, odd ones,

Poos that are hard, poos that are runny,

Ones that are boring, ones that look funny.

Whatever your poo is like,

However it smells,

Just love it to pieces,

It's from you, no-one else.

Pooem 1 Follow-up questions...

What kind of poos do you think your teachers or friends do?

Which are your favourite / least favourite types of poos to do?

Why not write some 'Pooetry' about them?

Or perhaps draw them with little poo faces on?

What is your favourite (and least favourite) place to do a poo?

Pooem 2: 'Who Dunnit?'
(A smelly classroom mystery)

There's a smell in the class!
But who could it be?
All I can say is,
It isn't me!

I wonder who it is?
It's time to find out.
Let's see who put this smell,
Out and about!

Abbey Ahmed sometimes toots when she's scared.
And Barry Barnes's nostrils look flared.
Colin Cooper blames Harry and Jem,
Though to be fair, it is often them.

Danielle Dunn, wind she rarely does break,
As for Emma Evans, one bad smell she can make.
Freddy Fox drops them whenever he shouts,
Is it Gary Gupta? I have my doubts.

Peter Allerton

Harry Hobbs smelt it first,

While Ibrahim Ince looks ready to burst.

Jenny Jones has a red face,

And Keisha King has just changed place.

Linda Lewis has a big smile,

She's been walking up and down the aisle.

Mrs Miggins, could it be you?

That would be too good to be true!

Nigel Nixon's just run away,

While Oliver Osman's been laughing all day.

Paul Powers seemed to make a rude noise,

It really could be one of those boys!

Quentin Quinn said he needed a dump,

Rachel Ratter looks too pretty to trump.

Sarah Smith could've let one go,

Was it Tina Tate? Well you never know.

Ursula Upton looks the type,

Wow, this smell really is ripe!

Vicky Veevers has just moved seats,

And Willy Watt's bottom sometimes bleats.

Xavier Xu has had cabbage for breakfast,

Zoe Zahn's butt is never the freshest.

As for me, my bottom can burp,

But a trouser cough? A botty chirp?

26 suspects,

I think it could be.

From A to Z,

Their names you can see.

But the trouble with smells,

Is they cannot be seen.

And to accuse me of one,

Well that would be mean.

Now let me see,

Who might it be?

Did you ever imagine,

It may really be me?

Well it could or it couldn't,

Who can possibly know?

But one thing's for sure,

I would never say so!

Pooem 2 Follow-up questions...

How many times, on average, do you think people make a smell every day? Can you find out?

How many different ways can you describe a 'fart'?

What was the most embarrassing smell you've ever made?

How do you feel if someone accuses you of making a smell, even if it really was you?

Can you write some 'Pooetry' about it?

Share your answers to the follow-up questions in this book - and discover more weird and wonderful stories - here:

www.peterallertonwriter.blogspot.co.uk

The End

Printed in Great Britain
by Amazon